In memory of my
father and mother
~ A. H. B.

To all my friends and my
dearest wife, Tiziana
~ J.B.

LITTLE TIGER PRESS
An imprint of Magi Publications
1 The Coda Centre, 189 Munster Road, London SW6 6AW, UK
www.littletigerpress.com
First published in Great Britain 2002
First American edition published by
Penguin Putnam Books for Young Readers 2002
This edition published 2010
Printed in China • LTP/1800//0154/0910
2 4 6 8 10 9 7 5 3 1

Mole, Mouse
and the Falling Star

A.H. Benjamin

John Bendall-Brunello

LITTLE TIGER PRESS

Mole and Mouse were
the best of friends.
They had fun together.

They shared everything.

They trusted each other completely,
even with their deepest secrets.

When one was sad
or not feeling well the
other was always there
to comfort him.

That's how much
they loved each other.
"I'm lucky to have
a friend like you,"
Mole would say.

"No," Mouse would
reply. "I'm lucky to
have a friend like *you*!"

One summer evening, Mole and Mouse lay side by side on top of a hill, gazing at the starry sky.

"Aren't stars beautiful?" sighed Mole happily.

"Yes," said Mouse, "and magic, too. They sometimes fall from the sky, you know. And if you ever find a fallen star, your wishes will come true."

"Wow!" said Mole. "Then you could wish for anything in the world, and you would have it."

"That's right," said Mouse dreamily. "Just imagine that!"

Mole and Mouse fell silent
for a moment, dreaming of
magic stars and all the things
they could wish for.

Just then, a shooting star zipped
across the sky. One moment it was
there, and the next it had gone.
"Did you see that?" gasped Mole,
sitting up.
"Yes, I did," cried Mouse. "It's a
fallen star, and I'm going to find it!"

Mouse scrambled to his feet
and scurried down the hill.
"Wait!" called Mole, racing after him.
"It's my star! I saw it first."
"No, I saw it first!" shouted Mouse.
"It's *my* star!"

When they reached the bottom of
the hill, Mole and Mouse started
searching for the fallen star. Each
one hoped he would find it first.
But neither did.

Perhaps the star fell
in the woods, thought
Mouse. "I'll go and
look for it tomorrow."

Mole stared toward
the woods, too. He
was thinking exactly
the same thing.

But they did not tell each
other, and they went back
to their homes without
even saying goodnight.

The next day before sunrise, Mole snuck out of his house and set off toward the woods.

A few minutes later, Mouse did the same.

Mouse and Mole spent the whole morning
in the woods, looking for the fallen star.
Once or twice they spotted each other.
But they pretended they hadn't.

Then, toward afternoon, Mole came
across a small patch of charred grass.
Maybe this is where the star had fallen,
he thought. But someone's already
taken it. It can only be Mouse!

A little later, Mouse came across the
same charred patch of grass. He thought
the star had fallen there, too.
"It's gone!" he cried. "And I bet I know
who's taken it. It has to be Mole!"

As darkness fell, both Mole and Mouse made their separate ways home, each feeling very angry with the other. They did not speak to each other again, except to argue.

"You stole my star!" Mole yelled.
"No, you stole my star!" Mouse
yelled back.
Mole didn't trust Mouse, and
Mouse didn't trust Mole.

So, Mole sneaked into Mouse's house to find the star . . .

and later Mouse looked through
Mole's window to see where Mole
had hidden it.
But neither found the fallen star.

The days rolled by, and summer was nearly over. Mole and Mouse grew lonely and miserable. They missed each other's company, the fun they used to have together, the secrets they had shared. They even missed the sad moments.

Mole can keep the star if he wants, thought Mouse. All I want is my friend back.

If I had never seen that star, Mouse would still be my friend, thought Mole.

Soon the fallen star became
just a sad memory—until
one day . . .

Mouse was climbing the hill when
he spotted a golden leaf, swirling and
twirling in the air.
"It's the fallen star!" he cried. "Mole
must have lost it. I'll catch it for him."
Not far away, Mole noticed Mouse
chasing after something that looked
like a star.
It's Mouse's star, he thought.
I'll help him catch it.

Up and up the hill ran Mole and
Mouse, until they reached the top.
But the leaf was already high in
the sky, glimmering in the autumn
sunshine. It swayed this way and
that, as if waving good-bye, and
then vanished altogether.

"The star has gone back to the sky," said Mouse.
"That's where it belongs," said Mole.
"Maybe it's for the best," sighed Mouse.
"I'm sure it is," agreed Mole.
There was a moment's silence.
"Anyway, we don't need a star. We have
each other," said Mouse.
"Of course we have," agreed Mole.

They gave each other a big hug, and
then lay back on top of the hill, feeling
the wind. With their arms and legs
stretched out, they looked just like two
furry stars.